This Orchard
book belongs to

....

....

D0183860

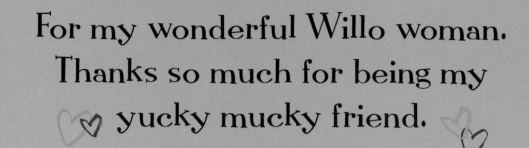

For my wonderful Willo woman.
Thanks so much for being my
yucky mucky friend.

ORCHARD BOOKS
338 Euston Road, London NW1 3BH
Orchard Books Australia
Level 17/207 Kent Street, Sydney, NSW 2000

First published in 2012 by Orchard Books

First published in paperback in 2013

ISBN 978 1 84616 948 9

Text and illustrations © Sam Lloyd 2012

The right of Sam Lloyd to be identified as the author and illustrator of
this book has been asserted by her in accordance with the Copyright,
Designs and Patents Act, 1988.

A CIP catalogue record for this book is available from the British Library.

1 3 5 7 9 10 8 6 4 2

Printed in China

Orchard Books is a division of Hachette Children's Books,
an Hachette UK company.
www.hachette.co.uk

Yucky Mucky Manners

Sam Lloyd

ORCHARD

Good morning!

I can't wait to meet the animals,
to smile and say hello.
Why don't you come and meet them, too?
Follow me, let's go.

I know that they'll be friendly
and terribly polite,

So, hurry up, join in the fun –
you'll see that I am right.

Oh . . . Gorilla's manners aren't really very good.
In fact he's acting badly, like a cheeky beastie would.
He pokes his finger up his nose and rummages about
And doesn't stop until he smiles and pulls a bogey out.

Here we see the zebra.
His stripes are black and white.
He's speaking with his mouth full
which is really not polite.

Just look at how he chats and chews
for hours and hours on end.
Yuck! Underneath that soggy food
you'll find his meerkat friend.

This parrot won't stop talking,
while his friend is trying to speak,
He just keeps right on squawking
from his pointy parrot beak.

Dear Parrot, please be quiet,
and listen to your chum,
Or else you might find yourself
inside a snakey tum!

Swinging through the trees with the warm wind in his hair,
This ape shows his botty . . . a botty that is BARE!

Although it's very pretty – pink, and squidgy, too –
It's really not the nicest way to say, 'How do you do?'

Crocodile scoffs his lunch.
He munches and he slurps.
He gulps and swallows, licks his lips,
then lets out smelly burps.
Errrrh! What is it that he's eaten?
It really smells disgusting!
Quick! Now let's get out of here
as crocs just aren't worth trusting.

Down beside the pool
there's a gentle jungle breeze.
Flamingo sniffs up lots of dust,
then does a great big SNEEZE!

She didn't cover up her beak,
that's really rather rude.
And, look, her sneeze has left her
friends completely in the nude!

Muddy pools are just the thing
that baby hippos love.
Squabbling to get in first,
they barge and push and shove.

What's happened to their manners?
They're jammed in there so tight,
That one pings high into the sky
and vanishes from sight.

Good grief! Oh, how nasty!
There's a horrid stinky smell.
This warthog hasn't had a wash
or cleaned himself too well.

His tusks are brown and crusty
and his fur is full of fleas.
Mrs Warthog pleads with him to
have a bath now, please!

Giraffe just munches leaves all day.
He loves to have a chew.
He's so busy eating – he forgets to find a loo . . .

So, whilst his head is in the clouds,
he ignores his 'other end'.
And, goodness me! Look at that!
He's pooped upon his friend!

The day is at an end,
and now it's turning into night.
And, look, here comes the elephant,
a creature who's polite!

But, hang on, what's that noise?
It's a gurgling, grumbling sound.
And can you feel those odd vibrations
rumbling through the ground?

Brrrummp!

A piercing parp escapes from Elephant's big botty.
I give up! I was wrong! ALL animals are grotty!

They trump along together –
they think it's funny when it's farty.
Jumping and pumping in a stinky parpy party!

What truly awful manners, a really shocking show.
Let's leave the creatures to it. It's time for us to go.

So, as we leave the jungle,
all that's left for me to say
Is that I'm glad us human beings
just don't behave that way!